For Janetta

Little Inchkin copyright © Frances Lincoln Limited 1994
Text and illustrations copyright © Fiona French 1994

First published in Great Britain in 1994 by
Frances Lincoln Children's Books, 4 Torriano Mews,
Torriano Avenue, London NW5 2RZ

www.franceslincoln.com

Distributed in the USA by Publishers Group West

First paperback edition 1995

British Library Cataloguing in Publication Data available on request

ISBN 0-7112-0917-0 (UK)
ISBN 1-84507-206-5 (USA)

Set in Palatino
Printed in China

9 8 7

LITTLE
INCHKIN

a tale of Old Japan

FIONA FRENCH

FRANCES LINCOLN CHILDREN'S BOOKS

Long ago in old Japan, Hana lived with her
husband Tanjo in a small house near a temple.
They both longed for a child.

One day Hana took gifts to the temple and
laid them before the great Buddha.

"Please give me a child," she whispered,
"even if it is only as big as a lotus flower."

A voice answered her. "Return home, Hana.
Your wish has been granted."

Not long afterwards, Hana had a beautiful baby boy.

"But he is so small!" she cried. "All the neighbours will make fun of me."

She and Tanjo named the tiny boy Inchkin. They took great care of him, but they did not love him.

The years passed by, and Inchkin grew up to be clever and brave.

But he was still no bigger than a lotus flower and this made him sad, for he longed with all his heart to be like other men.

One day he said to his mother, "I will go out into the wide world to make my fortune, and maybe I will find a way to grow as tall as other people."

Making a sharp sword out of a needle
and millet straw, and a strong suit of
armour out of beetles' wings, Inchkin
practised fighting crickets and
bumblebees, and even a big mouse.
He became a skilled swordsman.

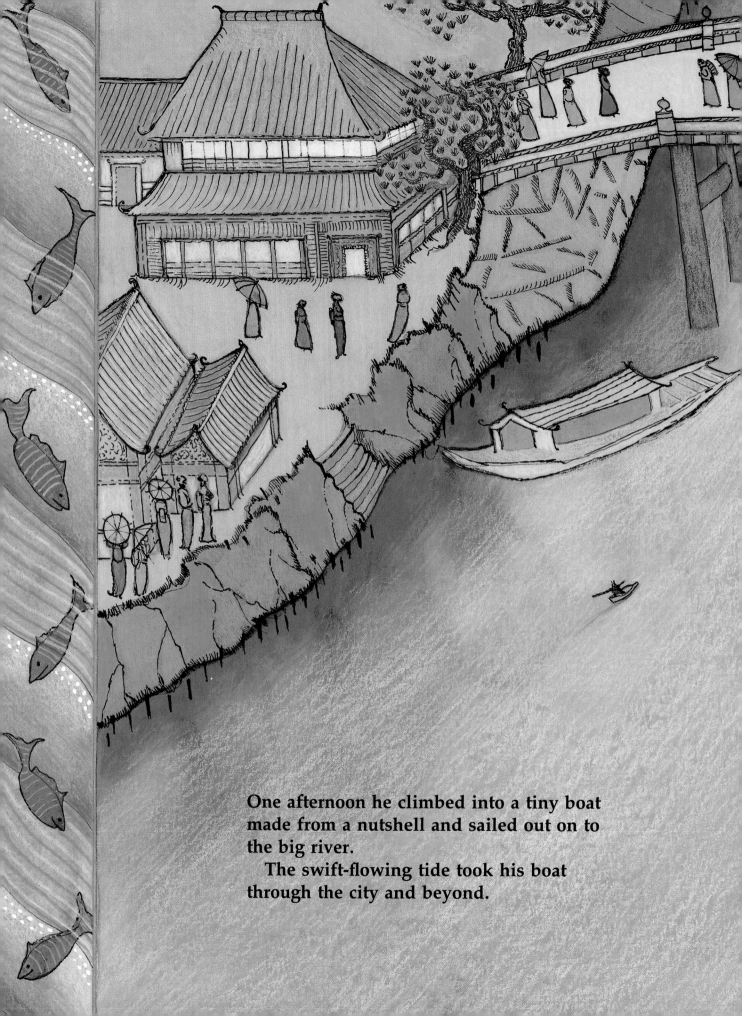

One afternoon he climbed into a tiny boat
made from a nutshell and sailed out on to
the big river.

The swift-flowing tide took his boat
through the city and beyond.

He had just reached the safety of a wide lake,
when a hand lifted him out of the water and
a voice high above him said, "Who are you?"
"I am called Inchkin," he replied. "I am one of
the best swordsmen in Prince Sanjo's land."

"I *am* Prince Sanjo," said the voice. "So you must prove to me how good a swordsman you are."

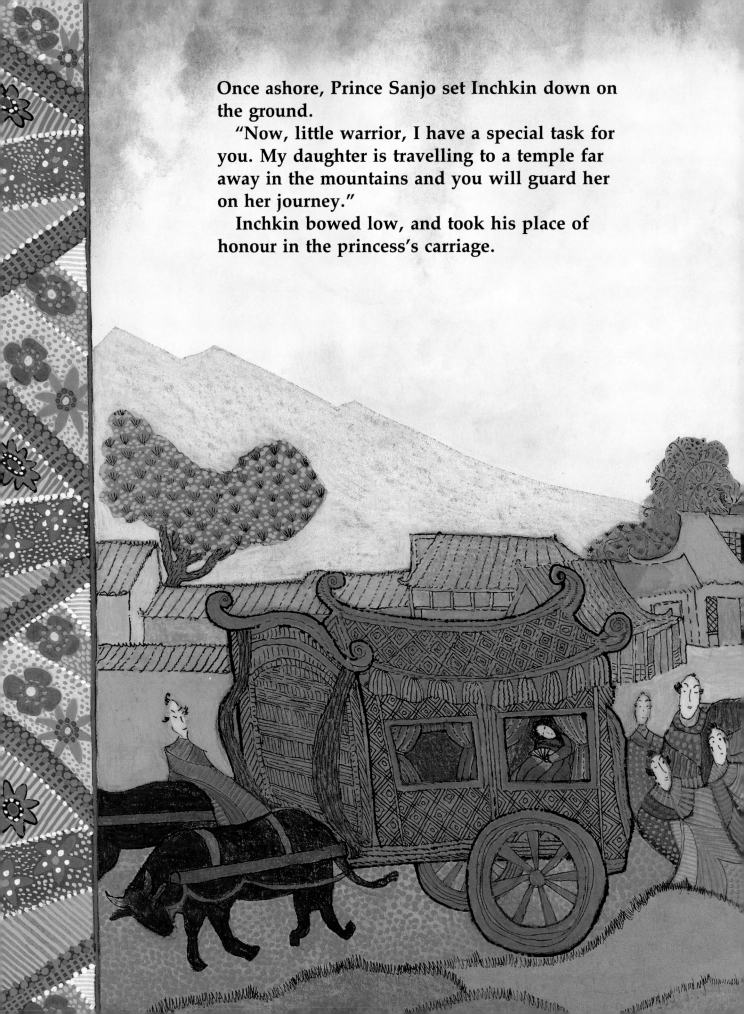

Once ashore, Prince Sanjo set Inchkin down on the ground.

"Now, little warrior, I have a special task for you. My daughter is travelling to a temple far away in the mountains and you will guard her on her journey."

Inchkin bowed low, and took his place of honour in the princess's carriage.

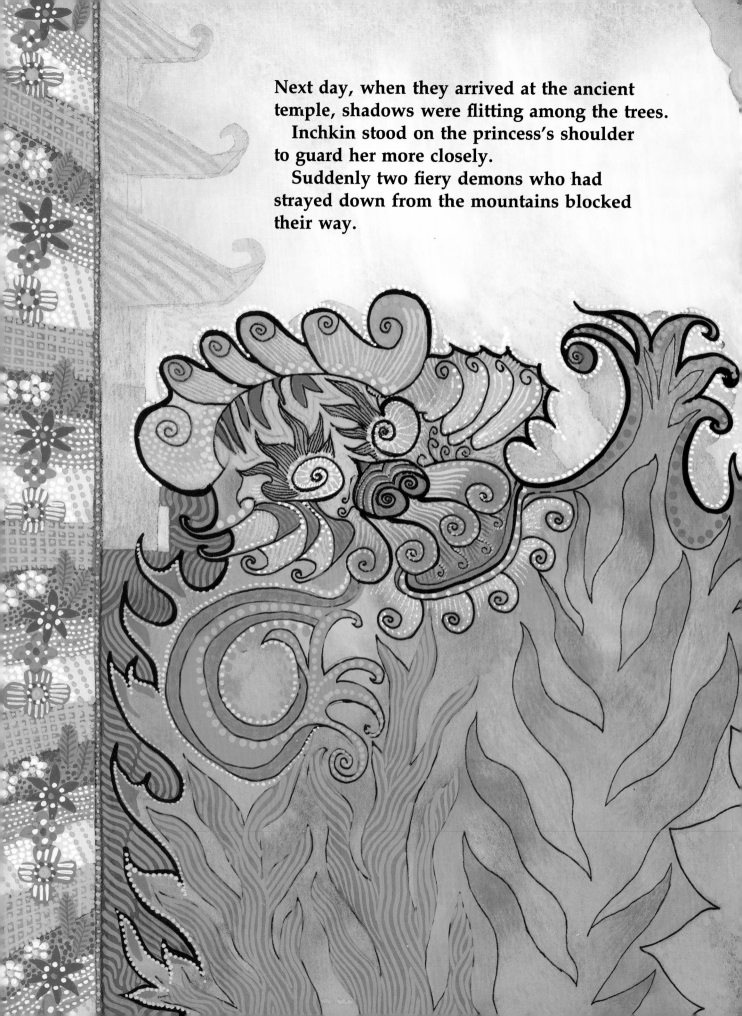

Next day, when they arrived at the ancient
temple, shadows were flitting among the trees.
　Inchkin stood on the princess's shoulder
to guard her more closely.
　Suddenly two fiery demons who had
strayed down from the mountains blocked
their way.

The princess went pale, but Inchkin gripped his tiny sword, ready to defend her with his life.

"Come any closer and I will kill you!" he cried.

The two demons were astonished.

One of them loomed over him. "You are very frightening," he sneered. "Why, I could eat you in one mouthful!"

Inchkin lunged at him with his sharp sword.

"Aieee!" cried the demon.

Before the other demon knew what was going on, Inchkin leapt between them. Shouting a fierce battle-cry, he swung his sword in the air and stabbed him hard in the nose.

The demon howled with pain and both the evil spirits fled away.

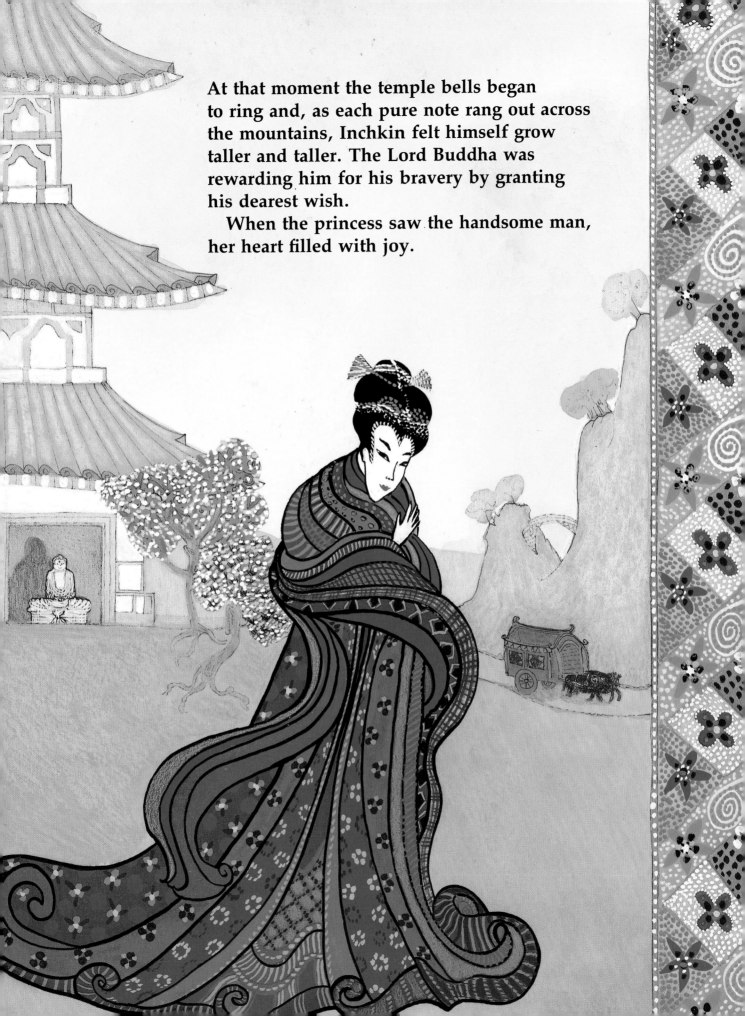

At that moment the temple bells began
to ring and, as each pure note rang out across
the mountains, Inchkin felt himself grow
taller and taller. The Lord Buddha was
rewarding him for his bravery by granting
his dearest wish.

When the princess saw the handsome man,
her heart filled with joy.

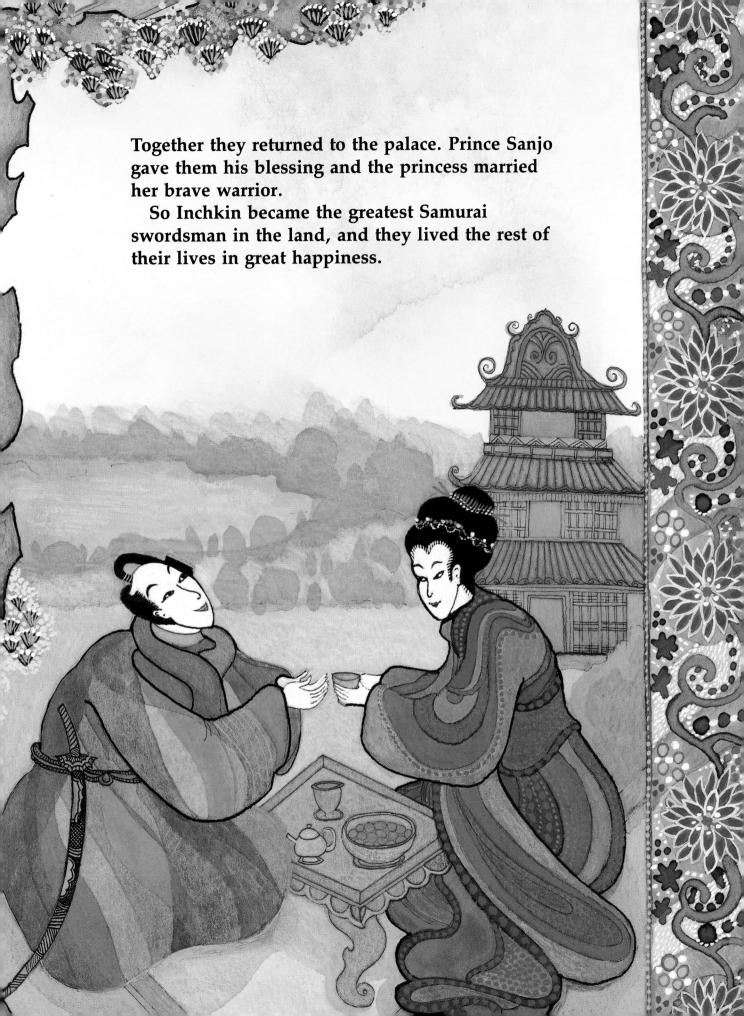

Together they returned to the palace. Prince Sanjo gave them his blessing and the princess married her brave warrior.

So Inchkin became the greatest Samurai swordsman in the land, and they lived the rest of their lives in great happiness.

MORE BOOKS IN PAPERBACK
AVAILABLE FROM FRANCES LINCOLN

Paradise

Illustrated by Fiona French

In seven days God created the universe, the world and its creatures.
They lived a perfect life in the Garden of Eden –
but one day, tempted by the serpent's seductive words,
Adam and Eve tasted the forbidden fruit
of the Tree of Knowledge.

The Glass Garden

Joyce Dunbar

Illustrated by Fiona French

When the wife of Lorenzo, the finest glassmaker in Venice,
dies of a terrible bee sting, he takes his daughter Lucia
away to live on a rocky island where there are no bees to sting –
but no birds or flowers either. Lorenzo builds an exquisite glass garden
where everything is silent and beautiful.
But time cannot stand still for ever…

The Emperor and the Nightingale

Meilo So

A striking new version of the famous
Hans Christian Andersen tale, beautifully retold
and accompanied by dazzling watercolour illustrations.
A delight to look at and read aloud.

Frances Lincoln titles are available from all good bookshops.
You can also buy books and find out more about your favourite titles,
authors and illustrators on our website: www.franceslincoln.com